The Berenstain Bears
VISIT THE DENTIST

Taking good care of their teeth
Is something all bears do.
That's why Sis and Brother brush—
And go to the dentist, too.

A FIRST TIME BOOK®

The Berenstain Bears VISIT

Random House New York

THE DENTIST

Stan & Jan Berenstain

One morning, Sister Bear woke up in the same old bed, in the same old pajamas, and yawned the same old yawn. But something was different.

"I have a looth tooth," she told Brother Bear.

"Well, push it back and forth with your tongue, and maybe it'll come out," yawned Brother, as he turned over to go back to sleep.

"Then what?" asked Sister. Brother had told her about the tooth fairy, and she wanted to hear it again.

"Then, put it under your pillow, and the tooth fairy will take it away and leave a new coin in its place. . . ."

"But," Brother added, "be sure to tell Mama about it first!"

Later, at breakfast, when Mama was reminding Brother that he had a dentist's appointment after school, she noticed that Sister was eating funny.

"She has a loose tooth," Brother explained.

"When it comth out," said Sister, wiggling it with her tongue, "I'm going to put it under my pillow for the tooth fairy."

"If she doesn't wiggle it out, she can come to the dentist with us and he can *yank* it out!" Brother grinned.

"Never mind that kind of talk," said Mama. "Dr. Bearson doesn't yank. He's very gentle and very careful."

"I'll get it out myself, Thmartie!" Sister shouted, as Brother hopped onto the big yellow school bus.

But Sister was still wiggling her loose tooth with her tongue when she and Mama met Brother after school and went to the dentist.

"Ith thtill thtuck," she said, showing Dr. Bearson her loose tooth.

"Well," said the dentist, "I'll have a look at it after I examine Brother's teeth. You can stand on this stool and watch—if that's all right with Brother."

"Sure," said Brother, as he climbed into the special cub's seat in the big dentist's chair. "She can watch me and see how it's done."

Brother had been to the dentist before, and he couldn't help showing off just a little.

Sister watched as Dr. Bearson checked each one of Brother's teeth with a special little tool.

"How do you see the backs?" she asked.

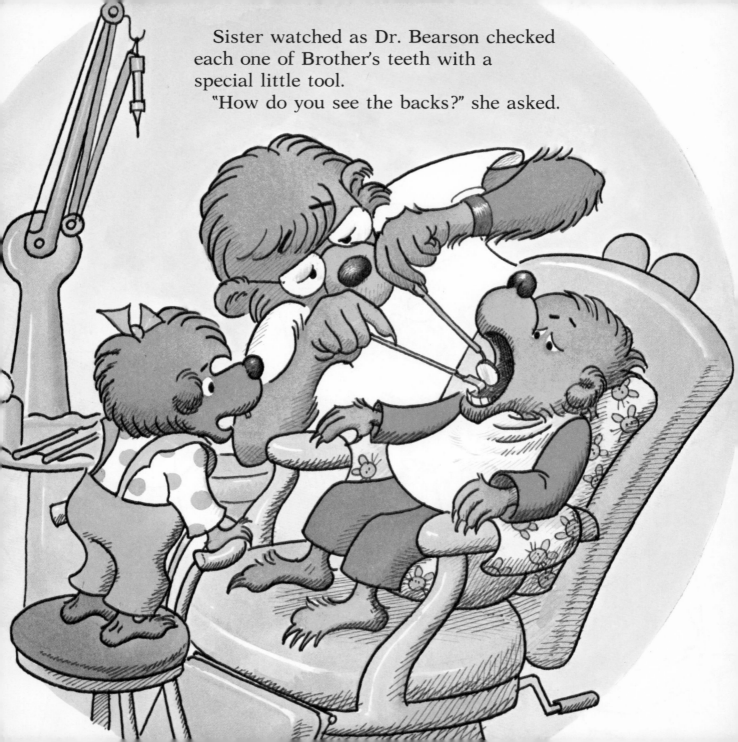

"With this little mirror," said the dentist. "Here. Have a look."

"Wow!" said Sister, looking into Brother Bear's mouth. "It looks like a cave. A cave with a tongue!"

While Dr. Bearson checked
Brother Bear's teeth, Sister
looked at the other tools on his
work tray—there were . . .

little picks, a scraper . . .

a tamper, and . . .

ULP!—a yanker!

She had become so interested
that she had forgotten all about
her loose tooth! She went to work
wiggling again. She wiggled hard.
But it was still stuck.

There were some other interesting
dentist's things:

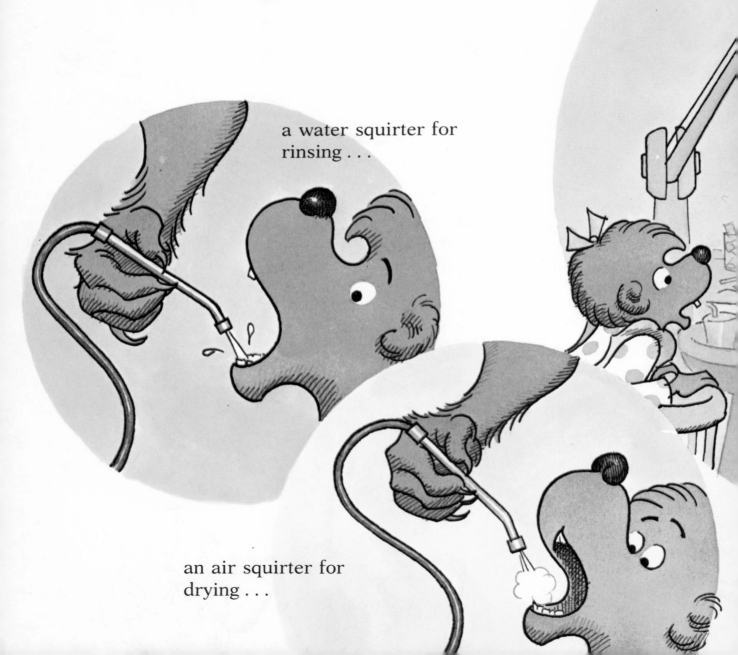

a water squirter for
rinsing . . .

an air squirter for
drying . . .

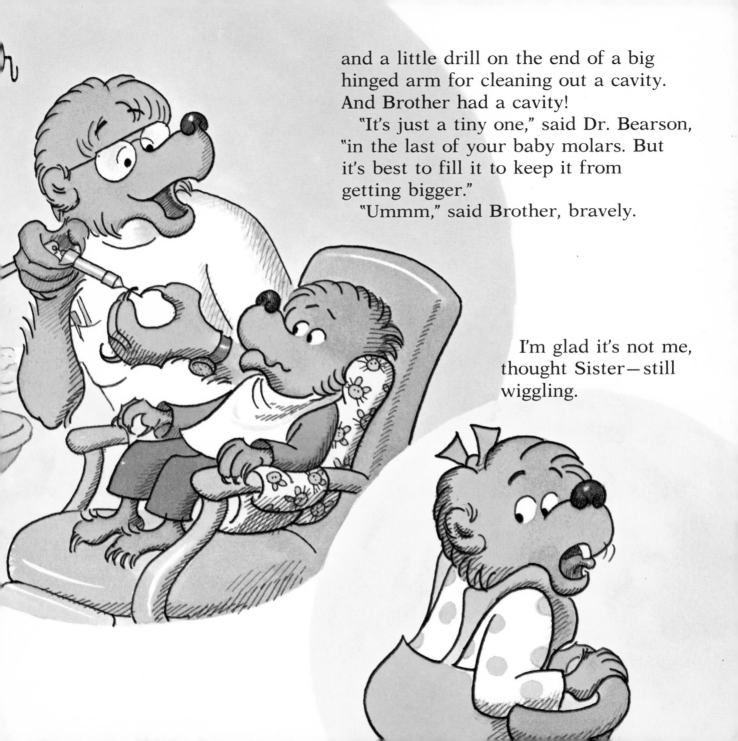

and a little drill on the end of a big hinged arm for cleaning out a cavity. And Brother had a cavity!

"It's just a tiny one," said Dr. Bearson, "in the last of your baby molars. But it's best to fill it to keep it from getting bigger."

"Ummm," said Brother, bravely.

I'm glad it's not me, thought Sister—still wiggling.

After Dr. Bearson cleaned out the cavity,
he rinsed it with the water squirter and
dried it with the air squirter.

Then he mixed up some
filling cement . . .

and filled it.

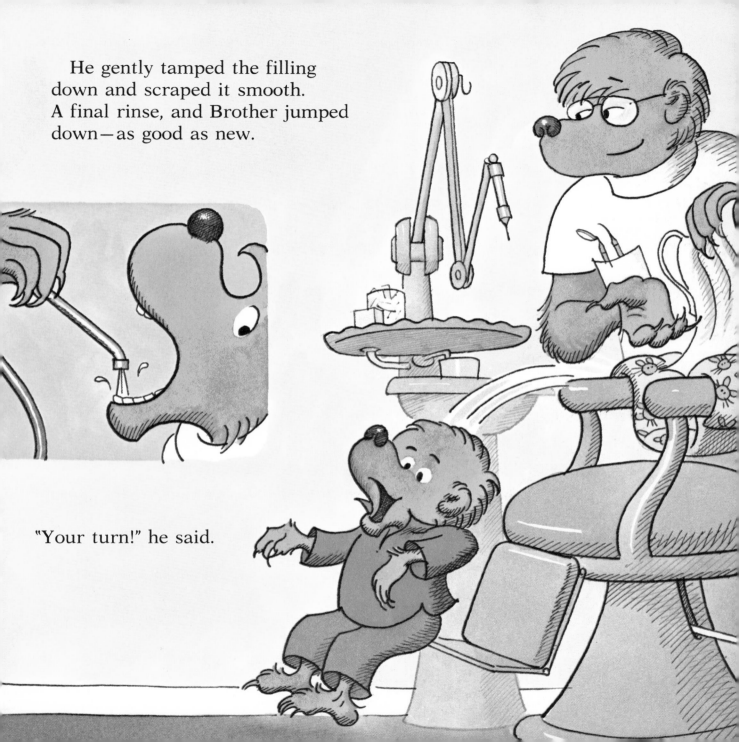

He gently tamped the filling down and scraped it smooth. A final rinse, and Brother jumped down—as good as new.

"Your turn!" he said.

Bravely, Sister climbed
up into the cub's seat—
still wiggling, but that
loose tooth just didn't
seem to want to come out.

"Hmmm," said the dentist, looking at the tooth.

"Ulp!" said Sister, waiting for him to reach for those big yankers. But while she waited, Dr. Bearson gripped the tooth with a piece of gauze, gave a tug, and . . .

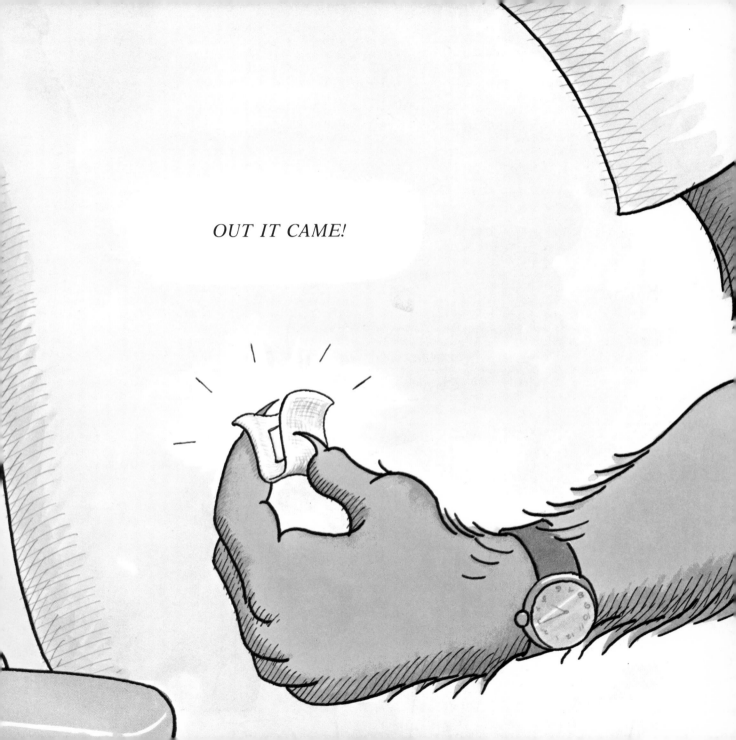

Sister looked at the tooth. It was very tiny. Dr. Bearson gave it to her to keep. Now it was her turn to hop down as good as new.

"Don't I get a lollipop or
something for being good?" she
asked Brother.

"You get a balloon," he said.
"Lollipops aren't good for your
teeth."

The next morning, Sister plunged her hand under her pillow and found a shiny new dime where the tooth had been.

"The tooth fairy came!" she told Brother.

"I told you she would," he yawned.